Presented To:

_____

From:

_____

On This Date:

_____

© 2017 Bible Belles
www.BibleBelles.com

Books may be purchased in quantity and/or special sales by contacting the publisher, Bible Belles, at hello@biblebelles.com.

Published in San Diego, California by Bible Belles. Bible Belles is a registered trademark.

Scripture quotations are from THE HOLY BIBLE, NEW INTERNATIONAL VERSION®, NIV® Copyright © 1973, 1978, 1984, 2011 by Biblica, Inc.® Used by permission. All rights reserved worldwide.

This book was created as a result of hard work, prayers, coffee, prayers, a lot of late nights, prayers, so much help from others, prayers, and a whole bunch of God's grace. Did we mention prayers?

Illustrations by: Megan Crisp

Interior Design by: Ron Eddy

Cover Design by: Rob Corley and Ron Eddy

Editing by: Julie Breihan

Printed in the United States

ISBN 978-0-9961689-4-6

Ruth
The Belle of Loyalty

written by
Erin Weidemann

illustrated by
Megan Crisp

Welcome, Little Belle.

Your superhero journey
begins right now…

"I can't believe it.

This cannot be happening!"

"It's okay, Dani. Don't cry." Rooney held her arms out, but it was no use. Dani was bouncing angrily around the girls bathroom. Her eyes were red and swollen.

"No, it's NOT okay! How can you say that?" Dani pressed her hands against her face and sobbed.

"How could my mom and dad not love each other anymore? My dad's moving out. Where am I even going to live?"

Rooney's eyes filled up with tears. *Dear God*, she thought, *please help my friend.*

"Hey, slow down. Let's pray about it," Rooney said gently, squeezing the golden bells on her bracelet.

"I don't want to pray with you right now. That's not going to do anything!" Dani glared at her.

Rooney lowered her head. "I only meant —"

"Ugh, just leave me alone," Dani said, backing away. "You're making it worse. I don't want your help."

All of a sudden the bathroom door flung open. There were Kylie and Maddie, standing in the hallway.

Oh no, Rooney thought in a panic. *What are you two doing here?*

"What's all this about?" Maddie laughed. "Why don't you just leave her alone, Rooney?"

"Yeah," Kylie agreed. "Let her breathe. Hey, Dani, why don't you come with us?"

Rooney stared at Dani. "I was only trying to help."

Dani shook her head. Then she turned and followed the girls out the door.

Rooney stood there, alone.

She clenched her fists. She tried to take a deep breath, but she couldn't. Her face felt hot, like it was on fire. She marched into the closest stall and slammed the door shut.

Rrrrrring!

Rooney heard a familiar noise. She lifted her head.

"Mari?"

Rooney saw a flickering light reflecting off the tile.

"I'm here," she heard Mari say. "Come out here and let's talk."

Rooney shook her head. "I don't want to come out. Did you see what Dani did? She just left with Kylie and Maddie. How could she walk away like that? I was only trying to help!"

She gritted her teeth. "If that's how she wants it to be, then fine. We won't be friends anymore."

Mari tapped the door gently. "Come on out of there."

Rooney wiped her eyes. She pushed open the door. The angel was waiting for her, hovering in the air.

"This is going to be hard for you to hear," Mari said as she flew down and squeezed Rooney's shoulder. "This isn't about you. It's about Dani."

"Her?" Rooney narrowed her eyes. "She's the one who was mean and left, not me! I was trying to help her, and she just walked out! She should come back and say she's sorry."

"Well, it's not really about that either." Mari held out her tiny hand. "Dani needs a true friend, and that's you, whether you want to be or not."

"How?" Rooney wanted to understand, but her feelings were hurt.

"Putting the needs of others before our own can be really hard sometimes." Mari hugged her. "It's time for you to meet Ruth."

Rooney reached for her bracelet. "Is she a Bible Belle too?"

Mari smiled. "Yes, and her power is the one you need right now. Are you ready?"

Mari flew close to the wall. She waved her hands over one of the mirrors. The glass began to ripple. Suddenly the reflection was gone. In its place was a wide, wooden window.

"Take a look."

Ruth 1

"See down there?" Mari pointed to an older man, walking with his wife. There were two young men following close behind.

Rooney watched the family walk slowly across a long stretch of land. "Is that Ruth?" Mari shook her head. "No, that's Naomi. She's married to Elimelek, and those are their sons, Mahlon and Kilion. They left their home in Bethlehem because of a great famine."

"Famine?" Rooney scratched her head.

"It's when there isn't enough food for people to eat," Mari explained. "They're going to another town called Moab to see if they can find food and live there together."

Mari nudged the window. Rooney could see Naomi and her two sons through the window of a little house. They were kneeling down together, and they were crying.

"Oh no." Rooney bit her lip. "Mari, what happened?"

"While they were living in Moab, Naomi's husband died," Mari explained.

"I can't believe my husband is gone," Rooney heard Naomi cry. "What am I going to do?"

Rooney closed her eyes. She squeezed the window frame tightly. *God*, she thought, *this is terrible! She must be so sad and lonely. How could this happen?*

Ruth 1

When Rooney opened her eyes, she could see the family inside the house. Two young women were with them.

"After her husband died, Naomi and her sons stayed in Moab. The boys married two young women from the town. That's Orpah," Mari motioned to a woman in a faded red robe, carrying a small plate of fruit. "And that's Ruth." Mari pointed to the woman in a beautiful blue robe. She moved gracefully across the room to fill a pitcher with water.

Rooney watched them for a while. "Maybe things will be better for them now."

"Well, they live together for almost ten years." Mari lowered her head. "Then Naomi's sons die too."

Rooney shook her head. "No!"

Mari bumped the window. Rooney could see Naomi, Orpah, and Ruth sitting inside the house.

"My daughters, my husband is gone, and my sons are dead." Rooney listened as Naomi spoke, her voice shaking. "There is no life for me here. Go back to your families. I will return to my home in Bethlehem."

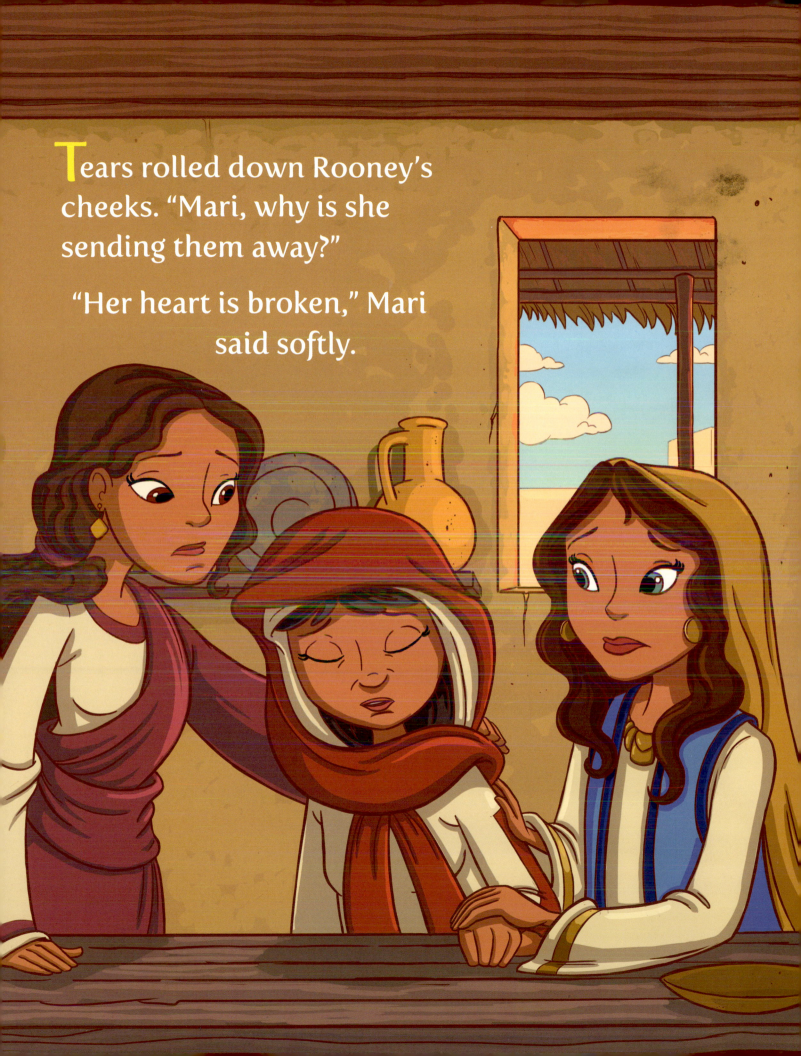

Tears rolled down Rooney's cheeks. "Mari, why is she sending them away?"

"Her heart is broken," Mari said softly.

"We will come with you," Ruth answered.

Orpah agreed. "Yes, we will go back with you to your people."

Rooney watched Naomi, Ruth, and Orpah pack up their belongings. She smiled as the three women set out on the road that would take them back to Naomi's home.

They walked for a while. Then suddenly, Naomi stopped.

"Go back," she said, trembling. "Both of you, go back to your home. May the Lord show you kindness, as you have shown kindness to your husbands and to me. Do not come with me."

Naomi covered her face with her hands.

"Go home, my daughters. Why would you come with me? Am I going to have any more sons who could be your husbands? Life for me is more bitter than I could have ever imagined. The Lord's hand has turned against me."

The three women cried together. Then Rooney watched Orpah stand up and kiss her mother-in-law. "Good-bye," she heard her whisper. Then she turned and started back toward the town.

Rooney squeezed her eyes shut.

God, she thought, *how can she just leave like that? Naomi's family is gone and she feels so alone!*

Rooney held her eyes closed for a moment. When she opened them, she saw Ruth. She had her arms wrapped around Naomi, holding her gently.

"Look," said Naomi, "your sister-in-law is going back to her people. You can go too."

Ruth placed her hands on Naomi's hands. She looked into Naomi's eyes. "Please," she said softly, "don't send me away. I will not turn my back on you."

Rooney grabbed the window. She listened as Ruth spoke.

"No matter what happens, I will not leave you. Where you go I will go. Wherever you stay, I will stay with you. Your people will be my people and your God my God. Where you die I will die, and there I will be buried. May God punish me, if I let anything but death separate you and me."

Rooney smiled for a moment, but her smile quickly turned down. She opened her eyes wide. Her heart began to pound. She sat down on the bathroom floor.

"Mari, no," Rooney said as she hugged her stomach.

"I can't do it. Dani was so mean earlier. She pushed me away. She doesn't even want to talk to me. I can't do what Ruth did." She shook her head. "I just can't do it."

Mari fluttered her wings in the air. Then she sailed down and landed on Rooney's knee.

"You can't do it alone," she whispered. "But, with God's help, you can do anything. Even this."

"But how?" Rooney looked back through the window. Ruth and Naomi were walking together down the road.

Mari put her tiny hand on Rooney's wrist. "Did you forget that you're a real superhero? You've got powers: prayer, patience, and bravery. And, best of all, you've got God. There's nothing you and God can't do . . . together."

Mari continued. "Tell God what's on your heart. Listen for His voice. He will guide you. Ask Him for the strength to do what is right. You've got to love Dani, no matter how she's acting."

"But why?"

"Because a true friend loves at all times."

Rooney took a deep breath. She folded her hands and closed her eyes.

"God, please, I need Your help. Dani hurt my feelings, and all I want to do right now is leave her alone. I know she must feel so sad and lonely, just like Naomi. Please help me to be like Ruth. Please help me be a true friend, even though Dani is pushing me away. I don't want to face her and the other girls after what happened, but I know You're with me. I know You will never leave me, no matter what."

Rooney paused. She thought quietly for a few moments.

"God? Please help me to love Dani like You love me."

Rooney stood up and poked her head out of the bathroom. She stepped carefully into the hallway. With the angel following close behind, Rooney turned the corner. Dani, Kylie, and Maddie were standing with a few other girls outside their classroom.

"I don't know if I can do this."

Mari squeezed her shoulder. "Remember, God is with you. He will help you."

"How can I tell if now is the right time?"

Mari leaned in and smiled. "It's really never the wrong time to do the right thing," she whispered.

Rooney looked at her, then back at the group of girls. *God, please move my feet*, she thought.

"Dani?"

Rooney's voice shook. "Can I talk to you for a minute?"

The girls looked at Rooney. They giggled. Rooney's heart sank.

Dani shrugged. "I don't really have anything to talk to you about right now."

Rooney's face felt red hot. "It'll just take a minute," she said gently.

"I guess. My mom's on her way to pick me up so it'll have to be quick."

Rooney nodded. The two girls walked across the hallway and sat down together on a bench.

Rooney folded her hands in her lap.

"I know you're angry about what's happening with your mom and dad. I know that you're hurting, and I'm so sorry you have to go through this."

She turned toward Dani.

"I want you to know that I love you and I am your friend, even if you don't want to be mine right now. I will always be here for you, no matter what. What happened earlier doesn't matter to me."

Rooney leaned in.

"I love you, and when you need me, I will be here for you."

Dani didn't say anything. She got up and stood there for a few seconds. Then she grabbed her backpack and walked away.

Rooney sat on the bench for a few minutes, thinking. Then she walked back over to where Mari was hovering, her head hanging low.

"I did it." She didn't look up.

"I know you're disappointed that this didn't go the way you were hoping, but you did it."

A tear fell down Rooney's cheek as she watched Dani get into her mom's car. She turned back to Mari.

"I just want my friend back."

Mari spun her hands in the air, and a bright, shining bell appeared. Rooney looked up as it floated into the air.

"Rooney, this is the Bell of Loyalty. Like Ruth, you have the power to put the needs of others ahead of your own. Ruth knew that Naomi was in pain and needed someone to love her. Ruth stayed with her, even though it meant leaving her home. Even when Naomi was pushing her away, Ruth chose to stay. That's exactly how God loves each one of His children."

Rooney nodded as the angel continued.

"God will never leave you. That is the real power: to love others faithfully, the way He loves you."

Rooney opened her hand as the golden bell floated down. It landed softly in her palm. She picked it up and looped it onto her bracelet.

"I want Dani to be my friend again. I just want things to be okay."

"Life isn't a fairy tale, Rooney. Sometimes, you don't get your 'happily ever after'. But God does have a very special plan for you. You are becoming the beautiful hero that He created you to be."

Rooney smiled a little. "Thanks, Mari. I gotta go. My mom will be here soon to pick me up."

Rooney walked out to the school parking lot. As she waited on the curb, Rooney looked down at the four shimmering bells that dangled from her wrist. She touched each letter with her finger.

"Hannah," she whispered to herself. "Esther, Abigail, Ruth —"

She stopped. Her heart began to pound. "H – E – A – R."

Rooney's eyes widened. She stared at her bracelet. Then she prayed.

God, what are You trying to tell me? What do You want me to hear? I'm listening! I know something special is happening to me. I can feel it. I'm changing. I don't understand it right now, but I know it's from You.

She looked up to the sky and grinned. From that moment she knew her life would never be the same.

A friend
loves at all
times.

— Proverbs 17:17

Check our website for free resources,
products and more books from
The Adventures of Rooney Cruz series.

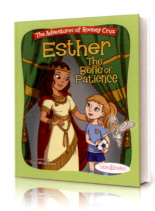

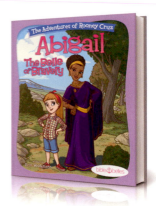

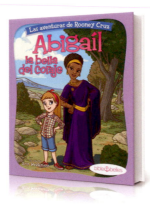

www.biblebelles.com
Heroes For Her

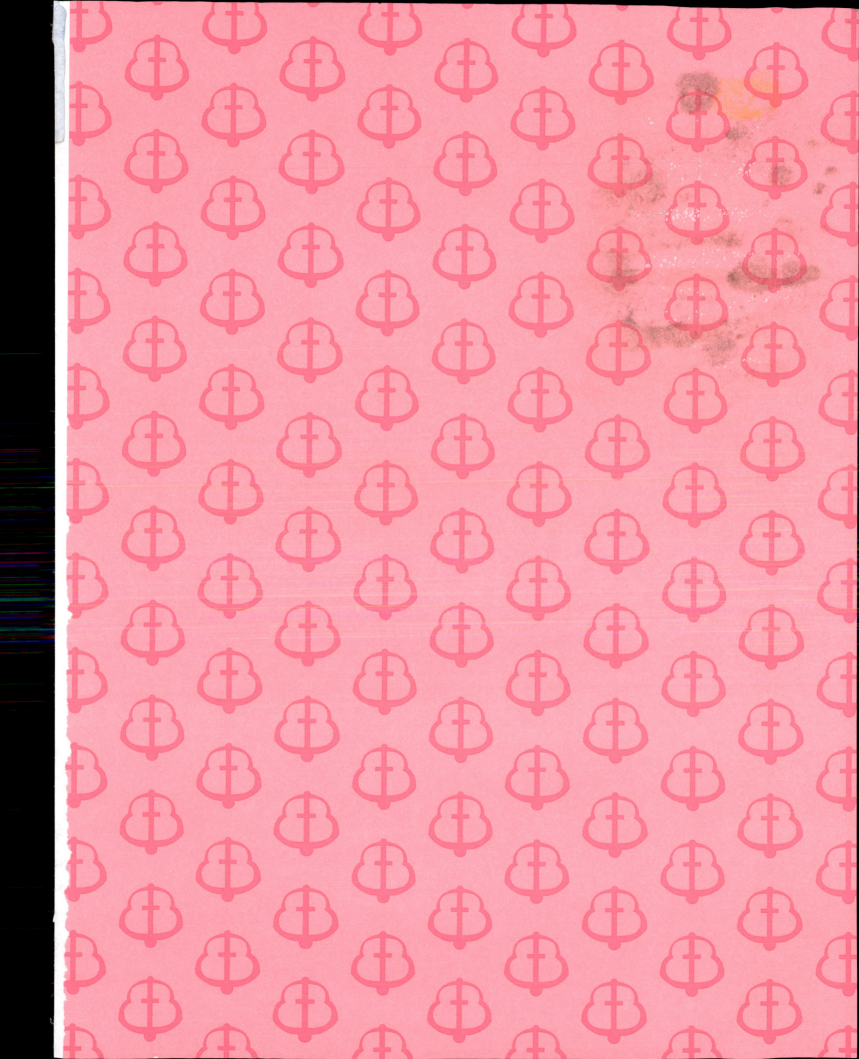